Come to the Meadow

Come to the Meadow

Anna Grossnickle Hines

Clarion Books

NEW YORK

FOR GRANNY

Clarion Books
a Houghton Mifflin Company imprint
215 Park Avenue South, New York, NY 10003
Copyright © 1984 by Anna Grossnickle Hines
All rights reserved.
For information about permission to reproduce
selections from this book, write to Permissions,
Houghton Mifflin Company, 2 Park Street, Boston, MA 02108
Printed in the USA

Library of Congress Cataloging in Publication Data
Hines, Anna Grossnickle.
Come to the meadow.
Summary: A little girl is eager to share the
delights of the meadow with her family, but everyone is
too busy until Granny suggests a picnic.
[1. Meadows—Fiction]   I. Title.
PZ7.H572Co   1984   [E]   83-14408
ISBN 0-89919 227-0

WOZ 10 9 8 7 6 5 4 3

"Come to the meadow, Mother.
Come to the meadow with me."

"It's full of monkey flowers and shooting stars

and little tiny buttercups."

"I can't today, Mattie. The ground is soft and I must plant the vegetables, pull the weeds, and tend the rosebushes."

"Come to the meadow, Daddy.
Come to the meadow with me."

"I saw a hoptoad down by the creek and

a pokey old turtle out taking a walk."

"I can't today, Mattie. The snow has melted and I must clean the cobwebs out of the shed, take down the storm windows, and put up the screens."

"Come to the meadow, Sister.
Come to the meadow with me."

"I found a bird's nest with three speckled eggs.

I'll show you if you promise not to touch."

"I can't today, Mattie. The air is warm and I want
to put up my hair, oil my skates, and fix the hole
in my kite."

"Come to the meadow, Brother.
Come to the meadow with me."

"The field mice made a tunnel under the grass and

the crickets are singing *cheer-up, cheer-up, cheer-up.*"

"I can't today, Mattie. The sun is shining and I have to find my baseball mitt, untangle this fishing line, and polish my bike."

"Come to the meadow, Granny.
Come to the meadow with me."

"I saw a spider spinning a web on a thimbleberry bush.

And the clouds look like vanilla ice cream."

"In the meadow? Spider webs and ice-cream clouds?

Oh, let's go see and take some bread and cheese
and hard-boiled eggs and apple juice..."

"And bananas?"

"Oh, yes, bananas."

"And cookies?"

"Especially cookies."

"And go to the meadow?"

"Straight to the meadow."

"And have a picnic?"

"Yes, a lovely, wonderful, delicious picnic in the meadow.

Because in the meadow..."

"IT'S SPRING!"